One day the wind wanted to have some fun.
She blew the hat off an Englishman.
It landed on a . . .

dog.

Next, the wind blew the hat off an Inuit.
It landed on a . . .

polar bear.

Next, the wind blew the hat off a nomad.
It landed on a . . .

camel.

Next, the wind blew the hat off a Mexican.
It landed on a . . .

donkey.

Next, the wind blew the hat off a cowboy.
It landed on a . . .

COW.

Next, the wind blew the scarf off an Indian.
It landed on a . . .

tiger.

Next, the wind blew the hat off an Australian.
It landed on a . . .

kangaroo.

Finally, the wind blew all these hats away,
and they landed on the . . .

moon.